Esmeralda loved everything about herself.

She loved her long black hair.

She loved the food that her mom made for her.

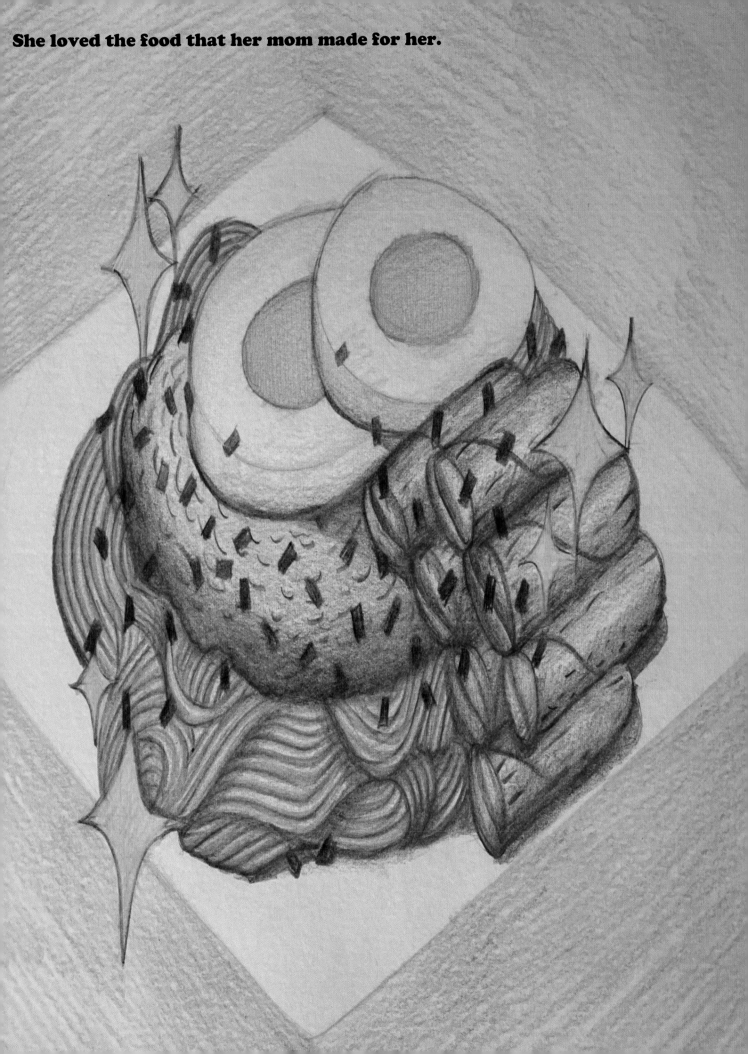

She loved the dress that her mom sewed for her.

On the first day of school, Esmeralda was excited to
make new friends.

At school, there would be so many people to meet.

She missed her friends from her old school in the Philippines.

This would be a new start, and Esmeralda couldn't wait!

At lunch time, Esmeralda sat at the first table she saw.

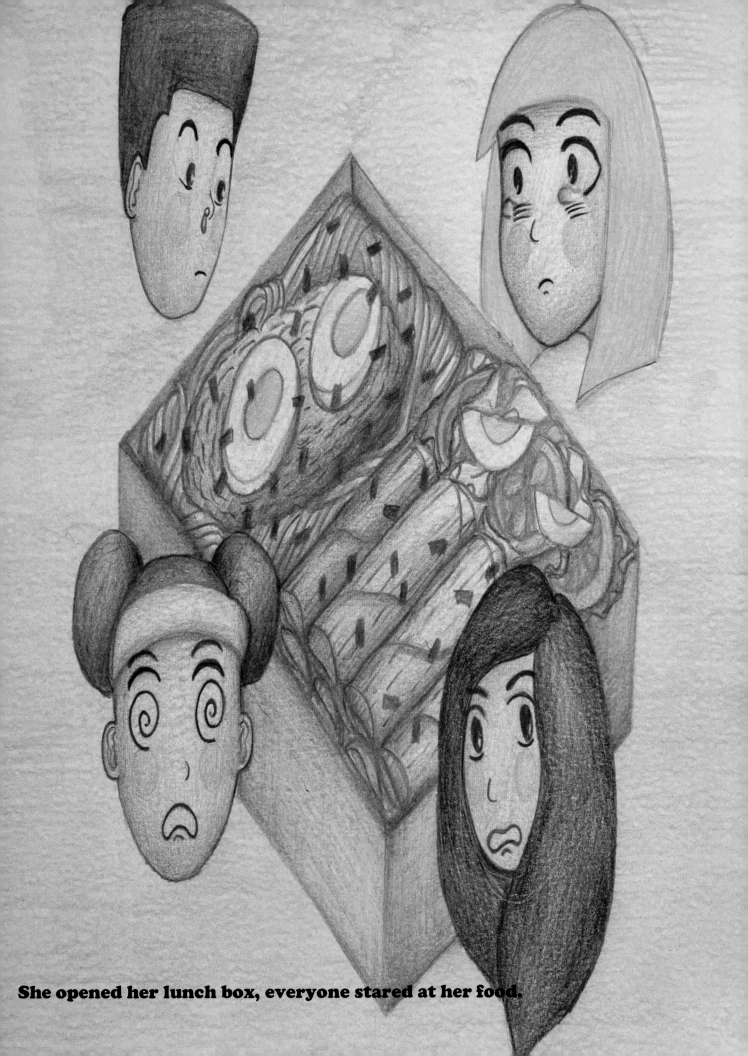

She opened her lunch box, everyone stared at her food.

"What is that?" a boy asked.
"Why does it look so weird?" said a girl.

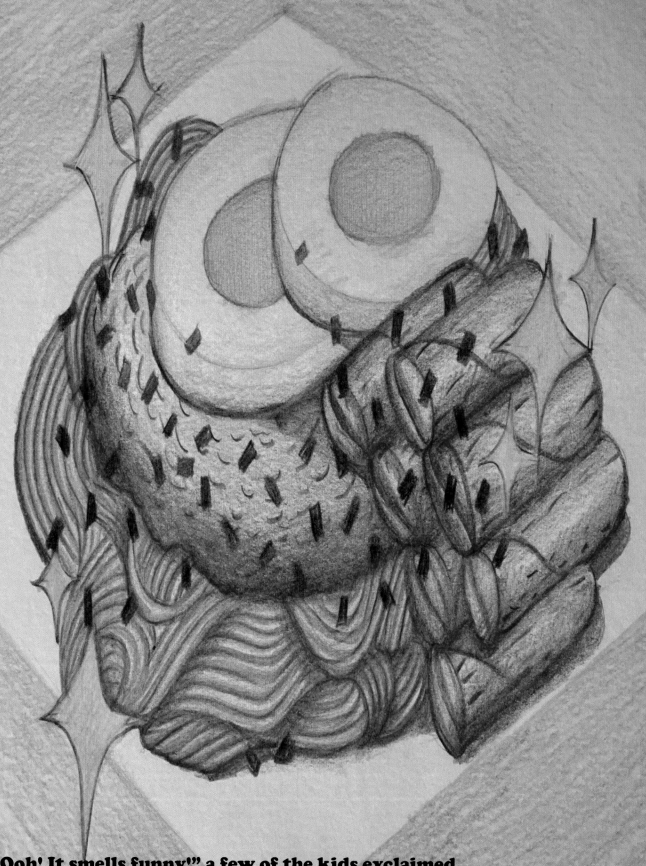

"Ooh! It smells funny!" a few of the kids exclaimed,
pinching their noses.

Esmeralda looked down at her feet and didn't answer.
She felt embarrassed.

When she got home, Esmeralda cried and cried.
She told her mom that she didn't want to go to
school anymore.

Dedication

For my mom, who is up in heaven and watching over us. We love you!

Esmeralda

Story by Michelle Armstrong

Illustrated by Michael Lansangan

Esmeralda loved everything about herself.

She loved her long black hair.

She loved the food that her mom made for her.

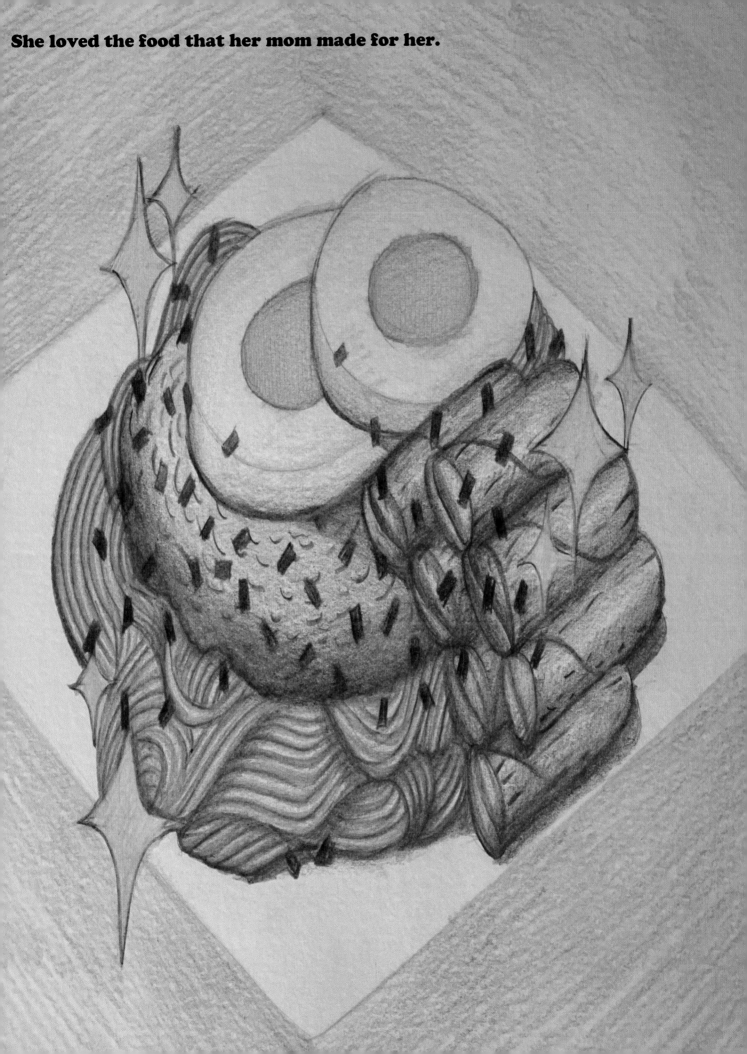

She loved the dress that her mom sewed for her.

On the first day of school, Esmeralda was excited to make new friends.

At school, there would be so many people to meet.

She missed her friends from her old school in the Philippines.

This would be a new start, and Esmeralda couldn't wait!

At lunch time, Esmeralda sat at the first table she saw.

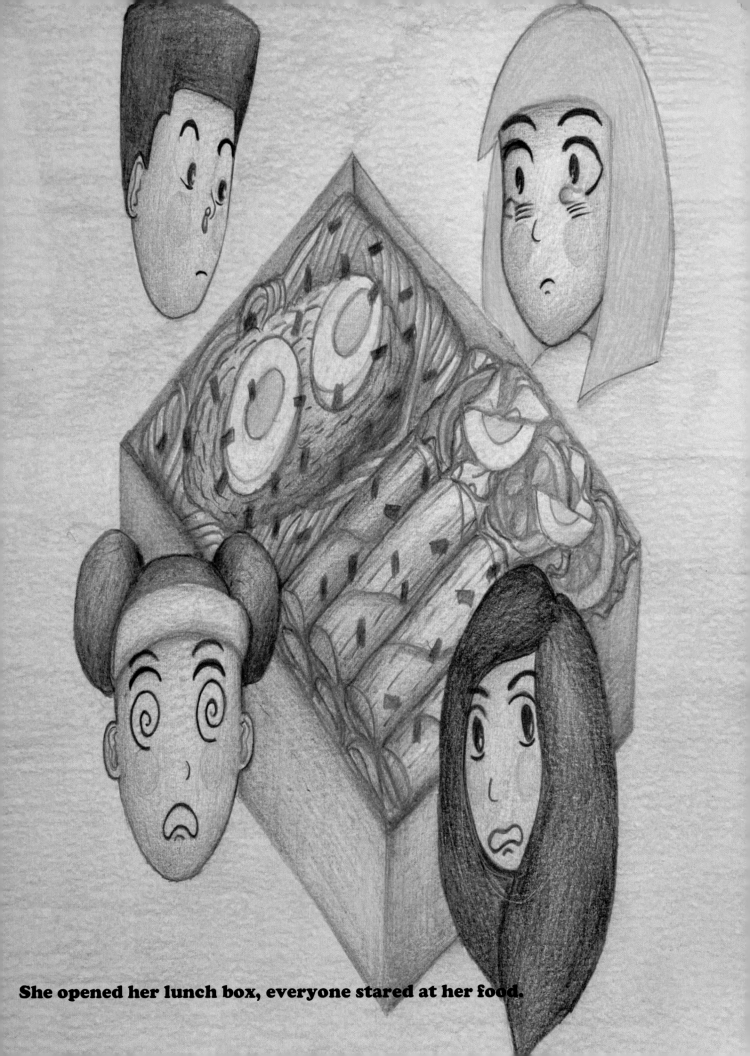

She opened her lunch box, everyone stared at her food.

"What is that?" a boy asked.
"Why does it look so weird?" said a girl.

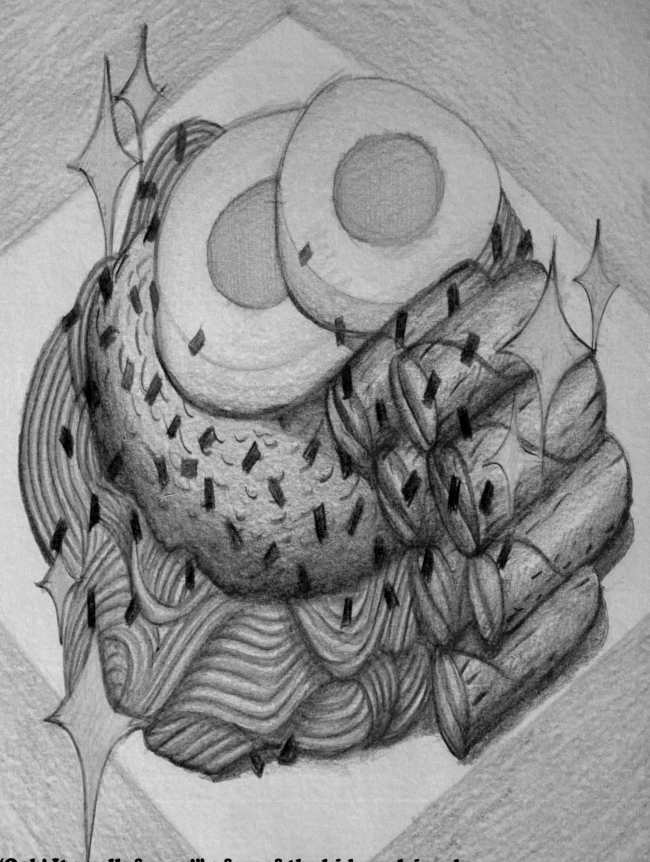

"Ooh! It smells funny!" a few of the kids exclaimed,
pinching their noses.

Esmeralda looked down at her feet and didn't answer.
She felt embarrassed.

When she got home, Esmeralda cried and cried.
She told her mom that she didn't want to go to
school anymore.

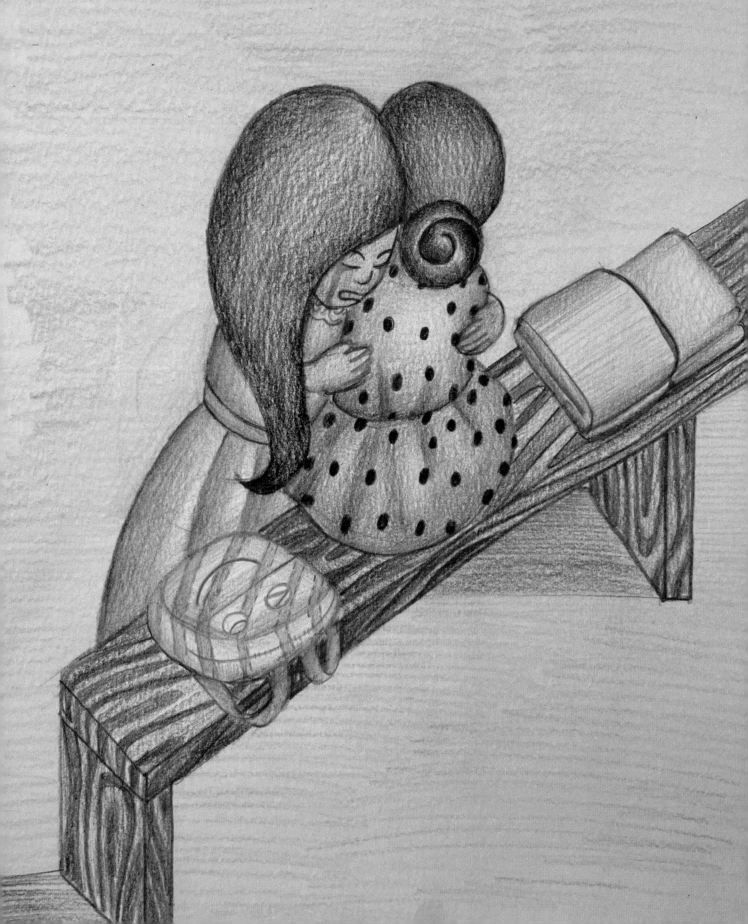

"The kids were mean to me," she said.
Esmeralda's mom hugged her. "It will be okay,
Esmeralda," she said. "Try again tomorrow."

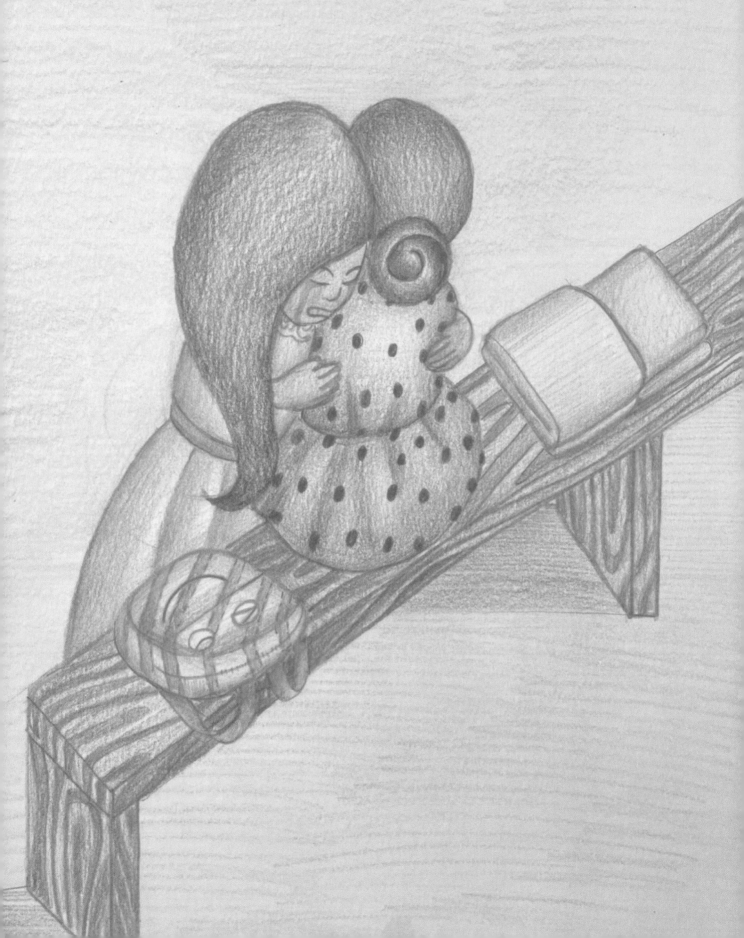

The next day during recess, many of the kids looked bored.

They had nothing to do.

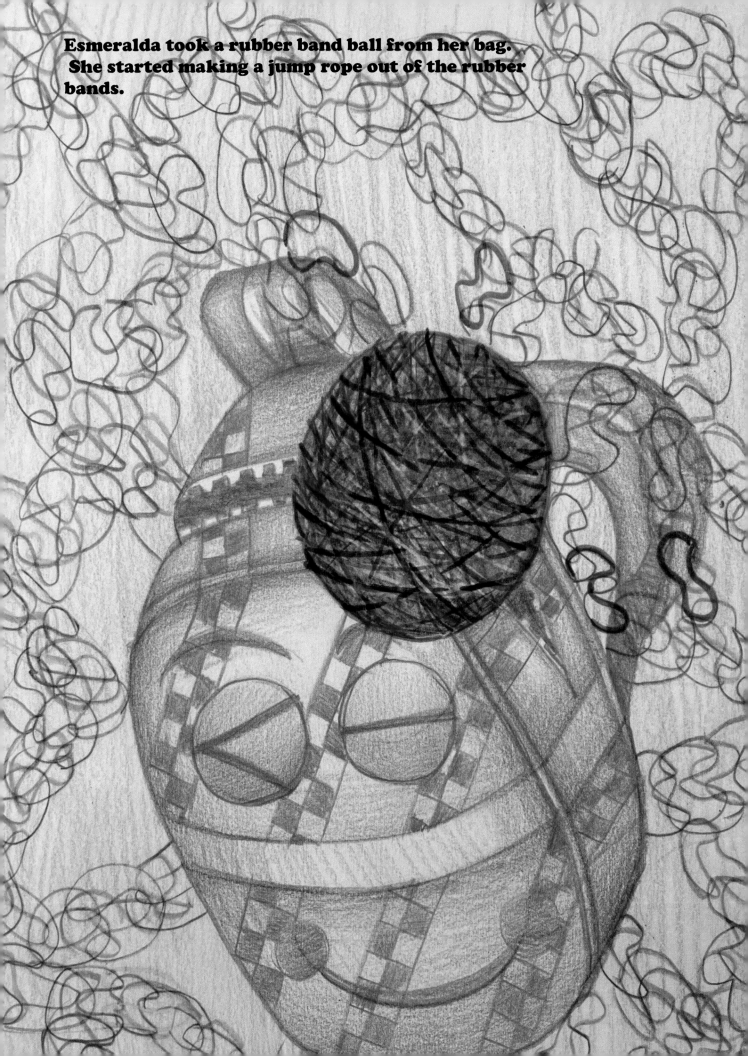

Esmeralda took a rubber band ball from her bag. She started making a jump rope out of the rubber bands.

She handed it to some of the other kids.
The kids were impressed.

"Good job, Esmeralda!" they called.

"You saved the day!" Esmeralda and the other kids skipped, jumped, and played.

"Let us teach you some jump rope rhymes!" the other
kids said happily. Then they began to teach Esmeralda.

From then on, Esmeralda loved her new school and all her
new friends.

Made in the USA
Monee, IL
16 January 2021

"The kids were mean to me," she said.
Esmeralda's mom hugged her. "It will be okay,
Esmeralda," she said. "Try again tomorrow."

The next day during recess, many of the kids looked bored.

They had nothing to do.

Esmeralda took a rubber band ball from her bag.
She started making a jump rope out of the rubber
bands.

She handed it to some of the other kids.
The kids were impressed.

"Good job, Esmeralda!" they called.

"You saved the day!" Esmeralda and the other kids skipped, jumped, and played.

"Let us teach you some jump rope rhymes!" the other kids said happily. Then they began to teach Esmeralda.

From then on, Esmeralda loved her new school and all her
new friends.

Made in the USA
Monee, IL
16 January 2021

Esmeralda

Story by Michelle Armstrong

Illustrated by Michael Lansangan

Dedication

For my mom, who is up in heaven and watching over us. We love you!